SONG OF FRANCIS AND THE ANIMALS

BY PAT MORA
WOODCUTS BY
DAVID FRAMPTON

EERDMANS BOOKS FOR YOUNG READERS

Grand Rapids, Michigan • Cambridge, U.K.

For my dear friend, Father Murray Bodo, O.F.M.,
a follower of St. Francis
— *P.M.*
To Natalie and Adrianne
— *D.F.*

Italian Phrases

Cantiamo — Let us sing.
Ti canto — I sing to you.
il lupo — the wolf

Text © 2005 Pat Mora
Illustrations © 2005 David Frampton
Published in 2005 by Eerdmans Books for Young Readers
An imprint of Wm. B. Eerdmans Publishing Company
255 Jefferson S.E., Grand Rapids, Michigan 49503
P.O. Box 163, Cambridge CB3 9PU U.K.

05 06 07 08 09 10   8 7 6 5 4 3 2 1

Library of Congress Cataloging-in-Publication Data
Mora, Pat.
The song of Francis and the animals / written by Pat Mora; illustrated by David Frampton.
p. cm.
Summary: Saint Francis of Assisi, friend to all creatures, sings with various animals.
ISBN 0-8028-5253-X (alk. paper)
1. Francis, of Assisi, Saint, 1182-1226--Juvenile fiction. [1. Francis, of Assisi, Saint, 1182-1226--Fiction.
2. Saints--Fiction. 3. Animals--Fiction.] I. Frampton, David, ill. II. Title.
PZ7.M78819So 2005
[E]--dc22
2004010240

The display and text type are set in Stempel Schneidler.
The illustrations were created as woodcuts.
Gayle Brown, Art Director
Matthew Van Zomeren, Graphic Designer

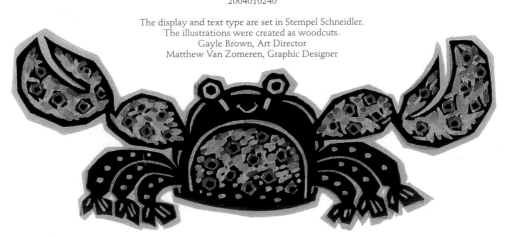

"Go play, my sisters. Go play,"
said Francis. He shooed away
the animals that followed him,
but the pheasant just peeked up
and walked on proudly, carrying the hem
of his brown robe in her beak.

"*Baa-baa*," sang the lamb.

"*Shoo*, go play," said Francis,

but the little lamb just grinned

and trotted happily behind the man

who preached to people and dogs

and flowers and fish and frogs.

"Where go you, brown brother?

Where go you?" Francis asked

the weary worm creeping,

creeping up the hot, rocky path.

Francis scooped the tired worm

and carried the curled worm gently

in his palm,

whispered a soft song

and placed the worm on a shady patch

of grass. The worm slithered

and slid into the cool greenness.

"Need a place to rest, my sisters?"

Francis called to the birds

flying and fluttering

round and round him.

His hands curved

into nests,

and a lark rested

on his head.

Robins nuzzled his dark beard.

Wrens, crows, and magpies landed

on his arms, twittering, cawing, and whistling

as if Francis were a safe, shady tree.

"Let's sing, my brother,"
a cicada called to Francis
from a fig tree.
"*Cantiamo.*"
The whirring rhythms
of Francis and the cicada
spun around the tree
and into the fruit,
sweetened the greenness,
fattened the figs
into soft, purple globes.

"Come, let's make the manger,"
said Francis to his friends.
On a cold December night
in a hillside hermit's cave
above the village of Greccio,
they dressed as Mary, Joseph,
and the quiet shepherds.

The ox and donkey stood still
as statues for hours
to help Francis.
They warmed the sleepy baby
with their steamy breaths.

Even the moon and stars hummed.
The lambs caroled
their lullaby, "*Baa-baa*."

"Why are you frightened, my brothers?"

whispered Francis to the people at Gubbio.

"The wolf!" they whispered. "*Il lupo.*"

They shivered at his hungry teeth

and red, growling, prowling eyes.

The wolf saw Francis and growled,

"*Grrrrrrrrrrrrrrrrrrrrrrrrrrrrrrr.*"

The wolf opened his mouth wide as
a cave and rushed toward Francis.

"Come let me pet you, my brother,"
said Francis, blessing the wolf.
Mouth open, teeth shining,

the wolf's paws suddenly dug into

the road, and the red-eyed wolf stopped.

He shuffled to Francis and placed his paw

on Francis's hand.

Francis patted the wolf, rubbed his hard jaw,

and the wolf patted Francis

with his tired paw.

"Wake me soon, Brother Falcon,

wake me soon," yawned Francis

as he curled up for a nap.

The falcon, like a devoted butler,

watched over Francis.

He watched Francis

breathing and dreaming.

When Francis was rested,

the falcon opened his beak wide

and called, "*Kek, kek, kek. Kek, kek, kek.*"

"Let's sing together, my sister,"

sang Francis to the nightingale.

"*Cantiamo.*"

As the sun set,

Francis and the nightingale

sang a duet

in their brown robes.

Their voices twirled

and whirled

over the rooftops

and over the hills

and over the world

like ribbons in the wind.

"I sing to you, Brother Sun.

I sing to you, Sister Moon.

"*Ti canto,*"

sang Francis resting

on a warm afternoon

under a leafy tree.

A hen clacked, "*Cluck, cluck, cluck,*"

and her chicks scurried

through swaying swirls

of poppies and buttercups.

They nestled around their brother

singing, singing

with people and dogs
and flowers and fish
and frogs.